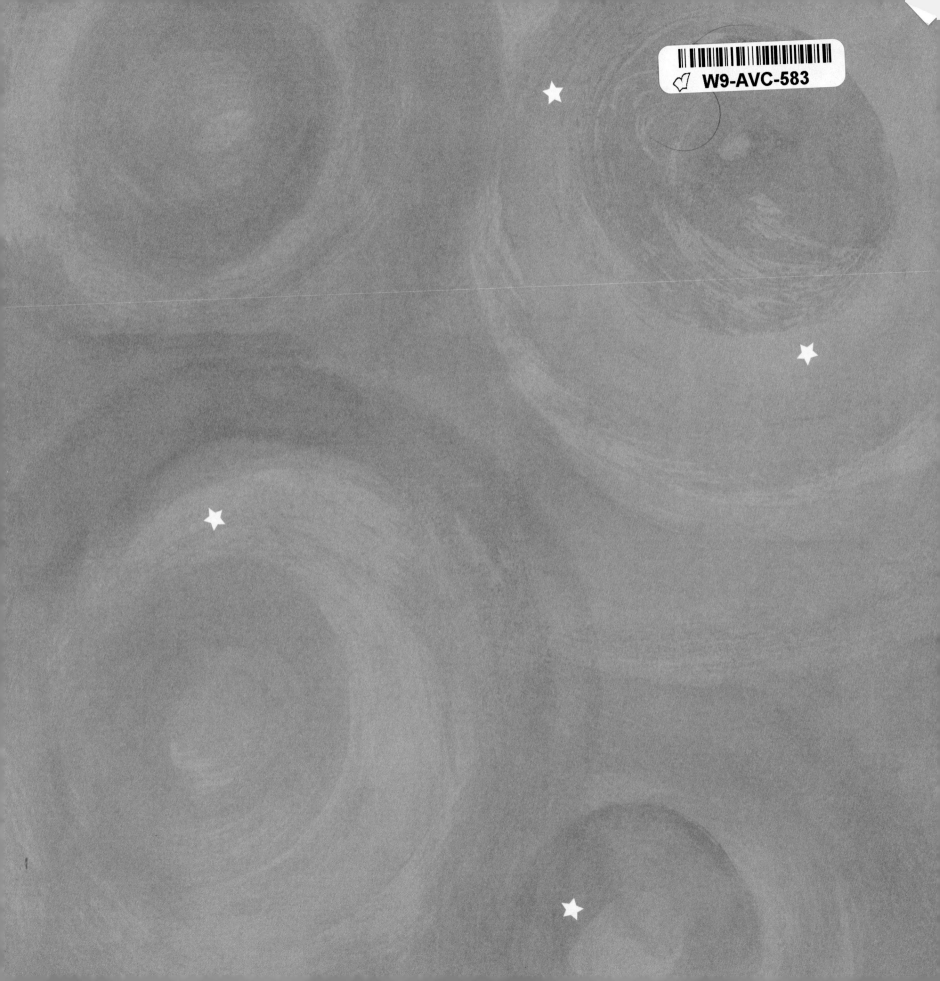

She is Born

is

A Celebration of Daughters

By Virginia Kroll

Illustrated by John Rowe

BEYOND WORDS Publishing INC

BEYOND WORDS PUBLISHING, INC.
20827 N.W. Cornell Road, Suite 500
Hillsboro, Oregon 97124-9808
503.531.8700 / 1.800.284.9673

She is Born

Text copyright ©1999 by Virginia Kroll
Illustrations copyright ©1999 by John Rowe

Edited by Marianne Monson-Burton and Michelle Roehm
Designed by Linda Warren and Laura Mische of the Warren Group, Venice, California

Distributed to the book trade by Publishers Group West

Printed in Hong Kong

LIBRARY OF CONGRESS CATALOGING-IN-PUBLICATION DATA

Kroll, Virginia L.
She is Born: a celebration of daughters / written by Virginia Kroll; illustrated by John Rowe.
   p. cm.
Summary: Baby girls are welcomed with different words, traditions, and possibilities in different cultures around the world.
ISBN 1-885223-94-3 (cloth)
[1. Babies—Fiction. 2. Girls—Fiction.] I. Rowe, John, ill.
II. Title.
PZ7.K9227Sg 1999
[E]—dc21
                                98-41585
                                CIP
                                AC

In celebration of
Sara Louisa, Hanna Grace, and Katya Mary, my daughters,
and of Olivia Hazel, my granddaughter.

—VIRGINIA

For my daughter, Julia, who is a continual delight and joy.

—JOHN

This book presented to:

From: _____

Date: _____

For a moment, everything hushes.

Then the balmy breeze whispers, "Sh, Sh…."

The ocean continues, "She is, she is…."

"…born

born

BORN!"

booms the thunder,

and Earth will never be the same.

Voices of

doctor

nurse

midwife

will mumble over

height and weight and wholeness.

She will be bundled in a

bark cloth blanket

kaross cape

knitted bunting

and hugged into belonging.

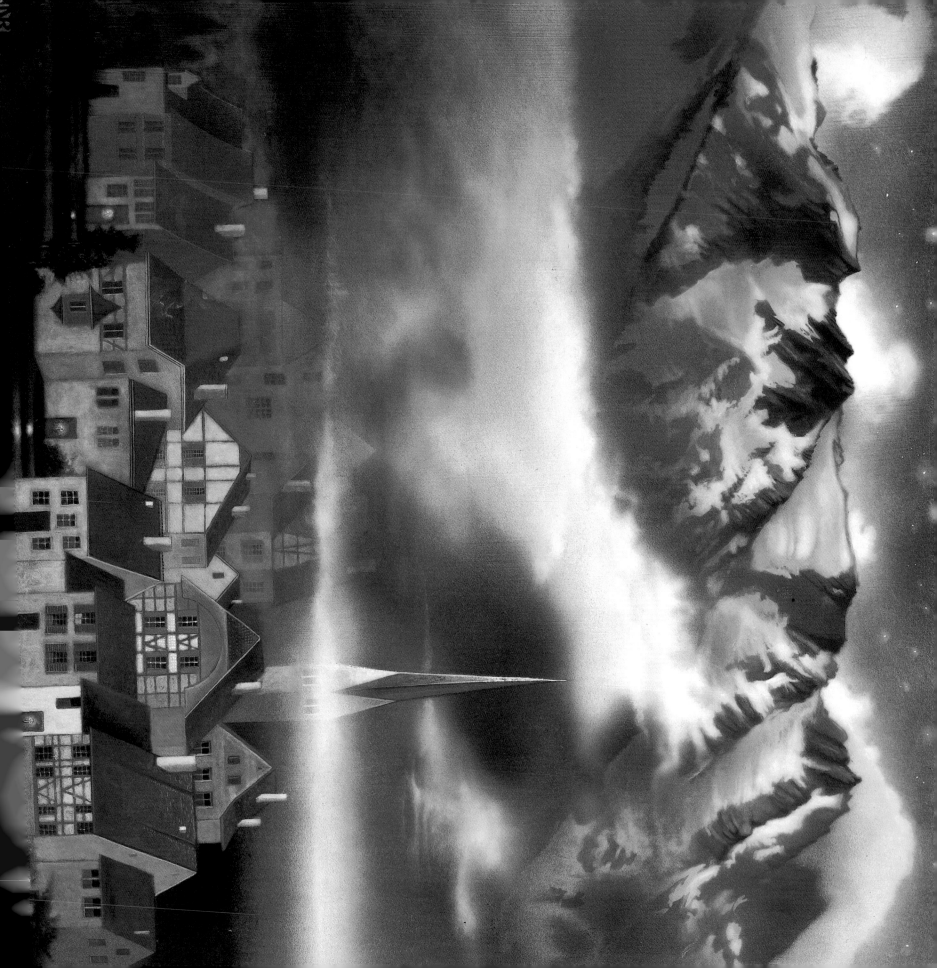

Her father will

hand out cigars

offer a beloved bullock

plant a cypress tree.

Others will welcome her with

pink balloons strung on porch railings

pink bows tied to doorknobs

animals drawn in the sand surrounding her home.

She will be

taken to a sacred cave

dipped in holy water

held up naked to the starlit sky.

In church temple grove of trees,
shaman priest rabbi will receive her,
pronouncing her name and
proclaiming her existence.

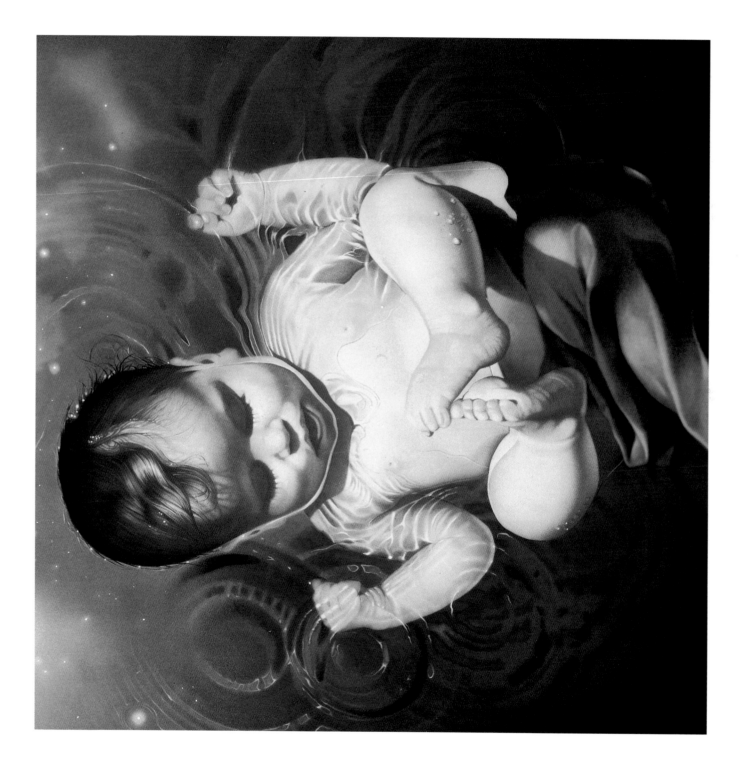

She will be called

Alena Bridget Carmen Dayo Erica Fatima Gina Hannah Isabel Jasmine Katya Louise Mu Lan Nanette Olivia Pinga Quaneisha Reiko Samira Tawny Ulani Virginie Winona Xanthe Yong Mee Zawadi...

...and given gifts of

dreamcatcher

carved soapstone seal

loops of ostrich eggshell beads.

At first with wide

gray   blue   brown   green   black eyes,

she will view the world from

amaut   lappa   rebozo

and in time her body will grow strong on

cornbread   rice   cakes

manioc porridge.

Her hands will

embroider delicate flowers onto festive clothing

twine vines into "letters" around her fingers

make maize into meal between metates.

Her feet will

kick SOCCER balls to victory across foggy fields

wade through racks of COCOa beans to dry them

dance to the rhythms of her uncles' drums.

Her head will harbor

memories of loved ones gone to their graves.

math facts

mythology

Her mouth will

sing remembered lullabies to littler ones

speak the languages of her sisters

on the other side of the globe

pray for crops to bloom and peace to grow.

She will be

daughter sister cousin

niece aunt friend wife,

and someday, maybe...

...she will feel the balmy breeze cool her wrenching pain

and hear the whooshing waves over her moaning

and yell for joy with the booming thunder,

"She is born!" while

"Mutter"

"Mère"

"Mamã"

echoes from the mountains,

and Earth will never be the same.

Author's Notes

PAGE 8

Bark cloth blankets are made by the Mbuti people of the Ituri rain forest in Africa by pounding the inner bark of fig trees with an ivory elephant tusk until the bark is softened. · Buntings are hooded sleeping bags knit out of cotton or wool, which were popular for North American babies in the 1920s. · A kaross is a leather cape often made from antelope hide by the Bushmen people of South Africa.

PAGE 10

In the United States, fathers traditionally hand out cigars to celebrate a child's birth. · Herders of East Africa, such as the Dinka and Masai peoples, love their cattle almost as much as they love their children. Only on a very special occasion, such as the birth of a child, is a cow sacrificed and its meat shared by the community in celebration. · In Israel, it is a custom to plant a cypress tree in honor of a daughter's birth. · In the United States, pink balloons are a traditional way to celebrate a daughter's birth. · In northern Europe, a pink bow on a door-knob signifies a girl's birth. · As a child is being born in Oaxaca, Mexico, a man might draw animals in the sand outside the family home. The animal he has finished drawing at the time of the actual birth becomes the child's *tona*, or animal guardian spirit.

PAGE 12

The Huichol people of Mexico make long journeys to sacred caves for their children's baptisms. · Many Christian sects baptize babies shortly after birth by pouring holy water over their foreheads or completely immersing them. Many other peoples also use water as part of their cleansing and naming rituals. · In several African societies, a newborn child is taken outdoors and presented to the four corners of the Earth.

PAGE 14

Alena (Russian), Bridget (Irish), Carmen (Mexican), Dayo (Nigerian), Erica (Scandinavian), Fatima (Portuguese), Gina (Italian), Hannah (Hebrew), Isabel (Spanish), Jasmine (Persian), Katya (Slavic), Louise (German), Mu Lan (Chinese), Nanette (French), Olivia (English), Pinga (Hindi), Quaneisha (African-American), Reiko (Japanese), Samira (Arabic), Tawny (Gypsy), Ulani (Polynesian), Virginie (Dutch), Winona (Native American), Xanthe (Greek), Yong Mee (Korean), Zawadi (Swahili)

PAGE 16

Dreamcatchers are web-like devices crafted by the Ojibwa Indians and hung above a child's sleeping place to ensure good dreams. · Eskimo artists carve figures of animals out of ivory or soapstone for their children. · The !Kung of the Kalahari Desert crush the shells of ostrich eggs to make beads for their babies' hair. These beads protect the children from harm.

PAGE 18

An *amaut*, worn on the back, is a decorated Eskimo baby carrier. A *lappa* is an African shawl, a *rebozo* is a Mexican shawl, and both are used as back or hip slings for carrying babies. · Cornbread and other corn products have long been popular staples of the Pueblo Indian peoples in the Southwestern United States. · Rice cakes originated in Southeast Asian countries. · In Africa they make porridge from the starchy manioc root.

PAGE 20

Embroidered blouses, aprons, and caps are part of the national dress in many Slavic countries. · The Pygmy peoples have no written language, but the women know how to form an elaborate system of "letters" out of thin, ropelike fibers. · *Metates* are grinding stones used by the Pueblo and Navajo Indian peoples in the Southwestern United States.

PAGE 22

Soccer is the national sport of many European and South American countries and is played throughout the world. · In Central America, girls and women turn coffee beans on racks in huge drying houses by "dancing" through them. · In most parts of Africa, people drum and dance. The Yoruba and Ashanti societies are especially famous for their "talking drums," which actually mimic human voices.

PAGE 24

In many Asian societies, ancestors are honored and even worshipped at sacred shrines inside each family's home.

PAGE 28

"Mutter" is the German word for mother. "Mamá" is Spanish and "mère" is French.